To Happy Mama-Bonnie

Happy Mamas

Happy Reading
&
Best Wishes

Written by Kathleen T. Pelley

Illustrated by Ruth E. Harper

CWLA
PRESS
Washington, DC

For Happy Babies Leo, Lilia, and Evie Rose,
and for my own grown up Happy Babies, Meghan and Róisín.

—K.T.P.

For my Sara and Josh, my 'Mum' Pauline
(who passed away while I was doing this book),
and all the Happy Mamas and babies in the Johnson family.

—R.E.H.

CWLA Press is an imprint of the Child Welfare League of America. The Child Welfare League of America is the nation's oldest and largest membership-based child welfare organization. We are committed to engaging people everywhere in promoting the well-being of children, youth, and their families, and protecting every child from harm. All proceeds from the sale of this book support CWLA's programs in behalf of children and families.

CHILD WELFARE LEAGUE OF AMERICA, INC.
727 15th Street NW, Suite 1200, Washington, DC 20005
www.cwla.org

CURRENT PRINTING (last digit)
10 9 8 7 6 5 4 3 2 1

Cover and text design by Marlene Saulsbury
Edited by Rachel Adams

ISBN: 978-1-58760-160-6
Library of Congress Cataloging-in-Publication

What makes
a Mama happy
at the
dawn of day?

Feeding her little ones
bundles of bamboo shoots to
munch and crunch in leafy forest dell.

Diving deep for a fishy feast
that wee ones gulp
with whiskery snouts,

then follow with
a flip flap floppy
honk of delight!

Tossing pancakes in the pan.
Serve the stack,
all sticky and sweet,
turns a sleepy head into...

a smiley face.

That's a — *my baby's belly's full*
kind of Happy Mama

What makes
a Mama happy
as the sun
begins to climb?

Teaching her joey
how to hop and leap
beyond the pouch,
scrape a spot in cool of shade
to doze and dream the day away.

Teaching her calf how to follow close, trunk'n tail,
spray and snorkel,
trumpet loud...
a jungle cheer!

Teaching her
tot how to
tiptoe close...

watch and
wonder...

huff and puff...
a dandelion wish.

9

That's a — *see how smart my baby is*
kind of Happy Mama

*What makes
a Mama happy
as clouds
shuffle by?*

Playing with her
little ones.
Tag the tail.
Loop the loop.
Swing and
swoosh.

Dip and dangle,
all a tangle,
in a topsy-turvy,
fun fandango.

Slide'n slither.
Wibble-wobble.
Teeter-totter.

Wings all wonky.
Skate'n skid...

oops a daisy!

Peek-a-boo. Skip to my Lou.
Nibble nosies. Tickle toesies.

That's a — *come play with me*
kind of Happy Mama

What makes a Mama happy as twilight glimmers?

Watching her little ones
fly from the nest...
soar up high
into a world beyond...

of tips and tops,
and airy
wispy wonder.

Watching her little ones
all a-waddle and a-paddle.
All a-dabble and a-dibble.
Splish! Splash! Splosh!

Off they sail with a "Quack! Quack! Quack!"

Watching her little one pick up baby brother,

brush him off,
wipe his tears,
cuddle close,
and kiss
him better.

That's a — *see my baby go*
kind of Happy Mama

*What makes
a Mama happy
at hush
of night?*

Making music
with her little ones.
Singing beneath a
starry desert sky.

A serenade for the
man in the moon, to make
him smile and light up the night.

Crooning owly lullabies.
Hushabye, Rockabye, "Twit Twoo!"
Whispering "Whoooo!
Whooooo! Whoooo!"

through the
deep dark woods.

Singing rub-a-dub-tub songs in
the bath, while blowing bubbles,
floating ducks and sailing ships.

That's a — *sing song singing*
kind of Happy Mama

But as the moon glows and the stars shine,
what makes all Mamas, from desert to jungle,

from forest to field, from land to sea,

happiest by far?

Having their little ones next to them,
tucked up tight,
all cuddled and kissed...

from tusk to tail,
from beak to claw,
from snout to paw,

...from head to toe.

That's a — *my baby's loved and happy*
kind of Happy Mama

Happy night, Happy Baby!
Happy night, Happy Mama!